W9-BJR-229

10/2017

Dear Parents:

Congratulations! Your child is taking the first steps on an exciting journey. The destination? Independent reading!

STEP INTO READING® will help your child get there. The program offers five steps to reading success. Each step includes fun stories and colorful art or photographs. In addition to original fiction and books with favorite characters, there are Step into Reading Non-Fiction Readers, Phonics Readers and Boxed Sets, Sticker Readers, and Comic Readers—a complete literacy program with something to interest every child.

Learning to Read, Step by Step!

Ready to Read   Preschool–Kindergarten
• big type and easy words • rhyme and rhythm • picture clues
For children who know the alphabet and are eager to begin reading.

Reading with Help   Preschool–Grade 1
• basic vocabulary • short sentences • simple stories
For children who recognize familiar words and sound out new words with help.

Reading on Your Own   Grades 1–3
• engaging characters • easy-to-follow plots • popular topics
For children who are ready to read on their own.

Reading Paragraphs   Grades 2–3
• challenging vocabulary • short paragraphs • exciting stories
For newly independent readers who read simple sentences with confidence.

Ready for Chapters   Grades 2–4
• chapters • longer paragraphs • full-color art
For children who want to take the plunge into chapter books but still like colorful pictures.

STEP INTO READING® is designed to give every child a successful reading experience. The grade levels are only guides; children will progress through the steps at their own speed, developing confidence in their reading.

Remember, a lifetime love of reading starts with a single step!

Visit us on the Web!
StepIntoReading.com
randomhousekids.com

Educators and librarians, for a variety of teaching tools, visit us at RHTeachersLibrarians.com

ISBN 978-1-5247-1690-5 (trade) — ISBN 978-1-5247-1691-2 (lib. bdg.)

Printed in the United States of America   10 9 8 7 6 5 4 3 2 1

nickelodeon

SHIMMER and Shine™

Magic Carpet Race!

by Delphine Finnegan

based on the teleplay "Zoom Zahramay"
by Dustin Ferrer

illustrated by Jason Fruchter

Random House 🏠 New York

The magic carpet
race is today!

Shimmer and Shine give
Leah her own carpet.
Now they can all race!

The genies and Leah
ride to the starting line.

Zeta wants
to enter the race.
She dresses up
as a genie.

At the starting line,
Princess Samira
reviews the rules.

The genies must fly
over the beach.
Then they must
swoosh through the
market and zoom to
the top of the island.

The first genie to cross
the finish line will win
the Racing Gem!

Shimmer, Shine, and
Leah are ready.

Zeta is
ready,
too.

Princess Samira
waves the flag.
The race begins!

Oh, no!

Leah's carpet does
not fly very fast.

Shine grants Leah's first wish.

Now her carpet flies much faster!

Zeta leads the race.
She pours a magic
potion over the beach.

Poof!

Twisty trees grow
and make a maze.
The girls are lost!

Shimmer grants
Leah's second
wish.

A sparkly path shows them the way out.

In the market, someone throws fruit at them!

It is Nazboo!
And there is Zeta!
Her genie disguise
does not fool them!

Leah makes her third wish.
Magic paddles appear
to whack away the fruit!

Zeta uses another potion.

The girls' carpets go wild!

Shimmer and Shine fall.

They land on Leah's carpet.

The friends need
to control the carpet.
First they swing
from a star.
Then they zoom to
the top of the island.

Next they
bounce off
a bottle.

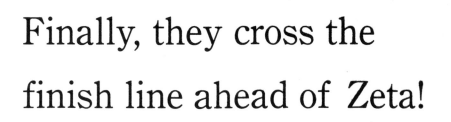

Finally, they cross the
finish line ahead of Zeta!

Leah, Shimmer, and Shine
win the Racing Gem!
It glitters and glows,
just like their friendship!